"Readers aren't born, they're made. Desire is planted—planted by parents who work at it."

—Jim Trelease
author of *The Read Aloud Handbook*

"When I was a classroom reading teacher, I recognized the importance of good stories in making children understand that reading is more than just recognizing words. I saw that children who get excited about reading and who have ready access to books make noticeably greater gains in reading comprehension and fluency. The development of the HELLO READING™ series grows out of this experience."

—Harriet Ziefert

Harriet Ziefert lives in Maplewood, New Jersey, and has taught children from preschool age up to 11-12 year-olds. She has written numerous books for children including NICKY'S NOISY NIGHT, NICKY'S PICNIC and WHERE'S MY EASTER EGG for very young readers, also published in Puffin Books.

Jill Bennett, who adapted the text for this edition, trained as a teacher and is now in charge of a reading centre near London. She is the author of several book guides including the highly acclaimed and influential LEARNING TO READ WITH PICTURE BOOKS.

PUFFIN BOOKS
Published by the Penguin Group
27 Wrights Lane, London W8 5TZ, England
Viking Penguin Inc., 40 West 23rd Street, New York, New York 10010, USA
Penguin Books Australia Ltd, Ringwood, Victoria, Australia
Penguin Books Canada Ltd, 2801 John Street, Markham, Ontario, Canada L3R 1B4
Penguin Books (NZ) Ltd, 182–190 Wairau Road, Auckland 10, New Zealand

Penguin Books Ltd, Registered Offices: Harmondsworth, Middlesex, England

First published in the USA in Puffin Books 1987
This edition published in Great Britain 1988

Text copyright © Harriet Ziefert, 1987, 1988
Illustrations copyright © David Prebenna, 1987
All rights reserved

Text anglicized by Jill Bennett

Printed in Singapore for Harriet Ziefert, Inc.

A New House for Mole and Mouse

Harriet Ziefert
Pictures by David Prebenna

PUFFIN BOOKS

"This is a nice house," said Mole.
"I like it.
   Let's try everything out."

"Okay," said Mouse.
"We'll try everything out."

First they tried the piano.

Music floated round
their new home.

Then they did some washing

and hung it out to dry.

They made a meal.
It was great fun.

But they did make a mess.

Next they had a bath.

The bath was fun, too.
But soap and water
went everywhere.

"I like this house," said Mole.
"Everything is terrific."

"Listen to the clock," said Mouse.
They listened as it went
tick-tock, tick-tock.

They went to the bedroom.
Mouse tried the bed.

Mole tried the light.
It went ON...

and OFF!

Mole and Mouse were tired.
Everything was quiet.
They went to sleep.

When they woke up,
they went downstairs.
Mole said, "I like this house.
Everything is terrific."

"But we haven't heard the doorbell ring," said Mouse.

They sat on the sofa
and waited for
the doorbell to ring.

They waited…
and waited…
and waited.

Suddenly the bell rang.
Ding-dong, ding-dong!
Mouse ran to open
the door.

Outside was a clown.
"Welcome to your new home,"
he said and gave Mouse
some balloons.

All of a sudden
everything was
not terrific!

"Help!" Mouse yelled.
"Help me! Quick!"

Mole grabbed the umbrella.
He popped the balloons.
Pop! Pop! Pop!

Mouse landed on the piano.

Plunk!

He was still holding a big red balloon.

Mouse and Mole laughed.
Everything was terrific again.